WRITTEN BY
CHRISTIANNE JONES

Sports Illustrated KIDS

ILLUSTRATED BY
HUSNA AGHNIYA

GOODNIGHT

Dance

CAPSTONE EDITIONS
a capstone imprint

The doors swish open. The crowd filters in.
It's almost time for the show to begin!

The theater is adorned with chandeliers of gold.
We find our seats—every ticket has been sold!

We page through our programs as they dim the lights.
It's going to be a memorable night!

The curtain slowly opens,
and the spotlight shines.

Ballerinas take the stage in two perfect lines.

The orchestra begins, and the ballet's underway!

The dancers stun with arabesques and pliés.

Dancing en pointe with buns in their hair,
the ballerinas look like they're floating on air.

Twirling and whirling in silk, tulle, and lace,

the dancers take you to a magical place.

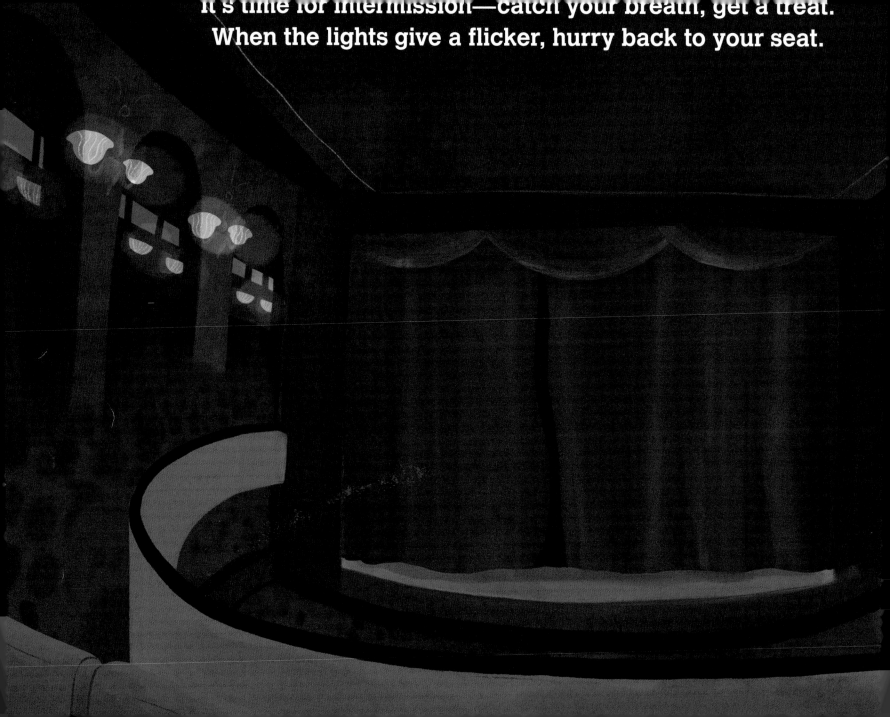

It's time for intermission—catch your breath, get a treat.
When the lights give a flicker, hurry back to your seat.

The prima ballerina does a grand jeté,
telling a wordless story that takes my breath away.

The music swells,
the excitement grows.

The dancers end in the perfect pose.

We all stand and cheer during curtain call.
Goodnight, ballet dancers. You gave it your all.

Goodnight, big stage. Goodnight, bright lights.
My dancing dreams have reached new heights!

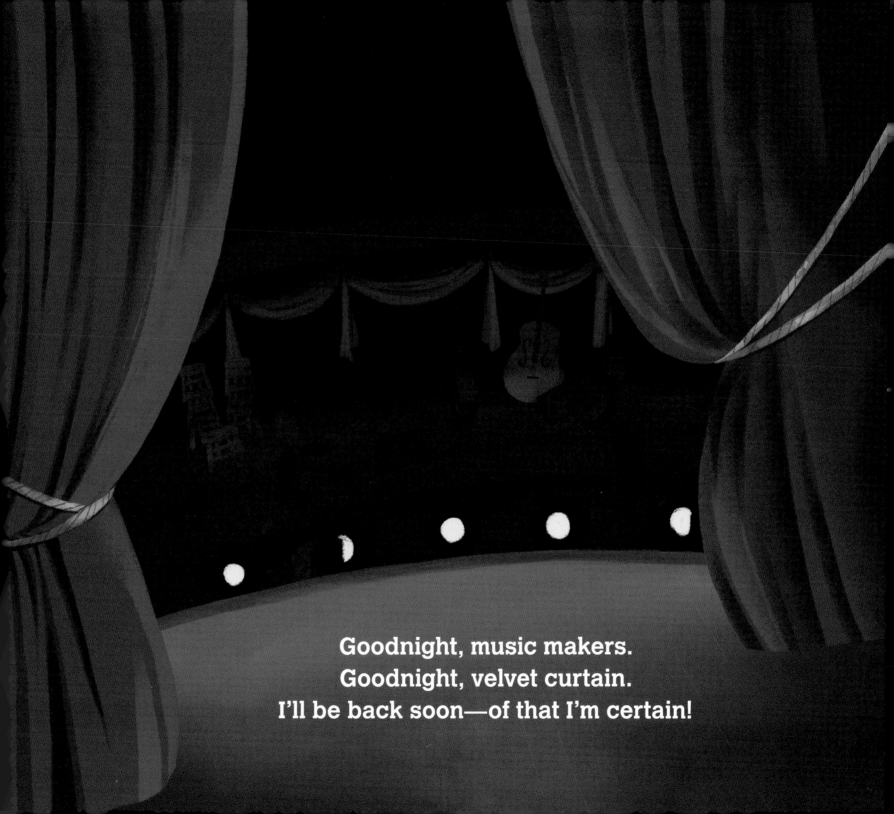

Goodnight, music makers.
Goodnight, velvet curtain.
I'll be back soon—of that I'm certain!

Goodnight, gorgeous costumes.
Goodnight, satin shoes.

One day I'll be onstage.
I'll be in the news!

Goodnight, happy crowd, who loved the show.

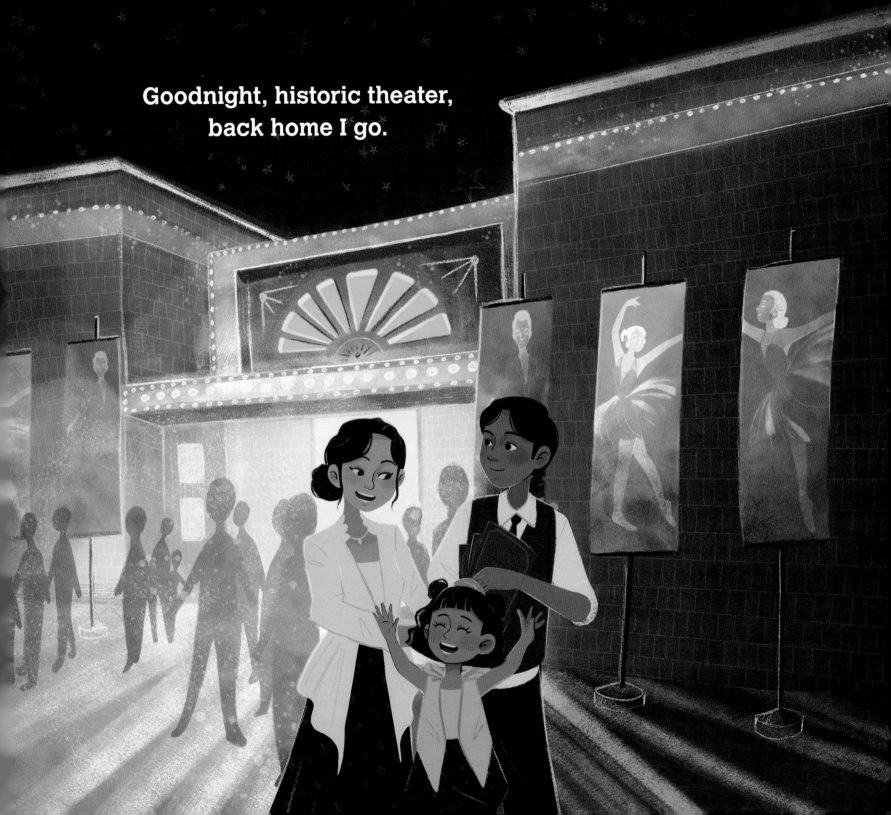

Goodnight, historic theater,
back home I go.

Goodnight, dance.
Goodnight, talented troupe.

Tonight I'll dream of my own ballet group.

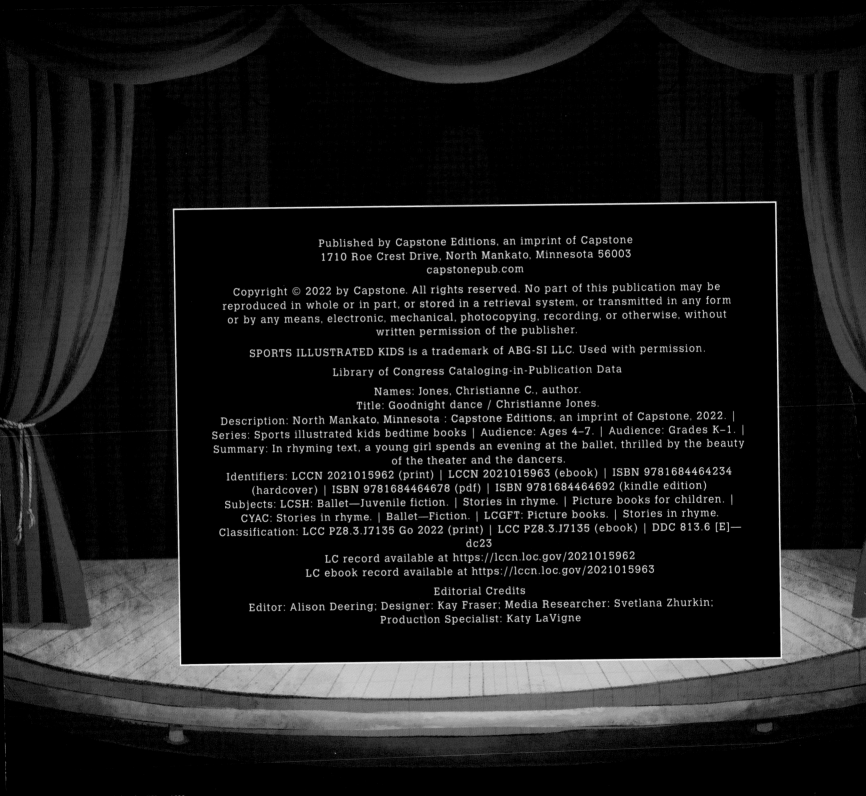

Published by Capstone Editions, an imprint of Capstone
1710 Roe Crest Drive, North Mankato, Minnesota 56003
capstonepub.com

SPORTS ILLUSTRATED KIDS is a trademark of ABG-SI LLC. Used with permission.

Library of Congress Cataloging-in-Publication Data

Names: Jones, Christianne C., author.
Title: Goodnight dance / Christianne Jones.
Description: North Mankato, Minnesota : Capstone Editions, an imprint of Capstone, 2022. | Series: Sports illustrated kids bedtime books | Audience: Ages 4–7. | Audience: Grades K–1. | Summary: In rhyming text, a young girl spends an evening at the ballet, thrilled by the beauty of the theater and the dancers.
Identifiers: LCCN 2021015962 (print) | LCCN 2021015963 (ebook) | ISBN 9781684464234 (hardcover) | ISBN 9781684464678 (pdf) | ISBN 9781684464692 (kindle edition)
Subjects: LCSH: Ballet—Juvenile fiction. | Stories in rhyme. | Picture books for children. | CYAC: Stories in rhyme. | Ballet—Fiction. | LCGFT: Picture books. | Stories in rhyme.
Classification: LCC PZ8.3.J7135 Go 2022 (print) | LCC PZ8.3.J7135 (ebook) | DDC 813.6 [E]—dc23
LC record available at https://lccn.loc.gov/2021015962
LC ebook record available at https://lccn.loc.gov/2021015963

Editorial Credits
Editor: Alison Deering; Designer: Kay Fraser; Media Researcher: Svetlana Zhurkin; Production Specialist: Katy LaVigne

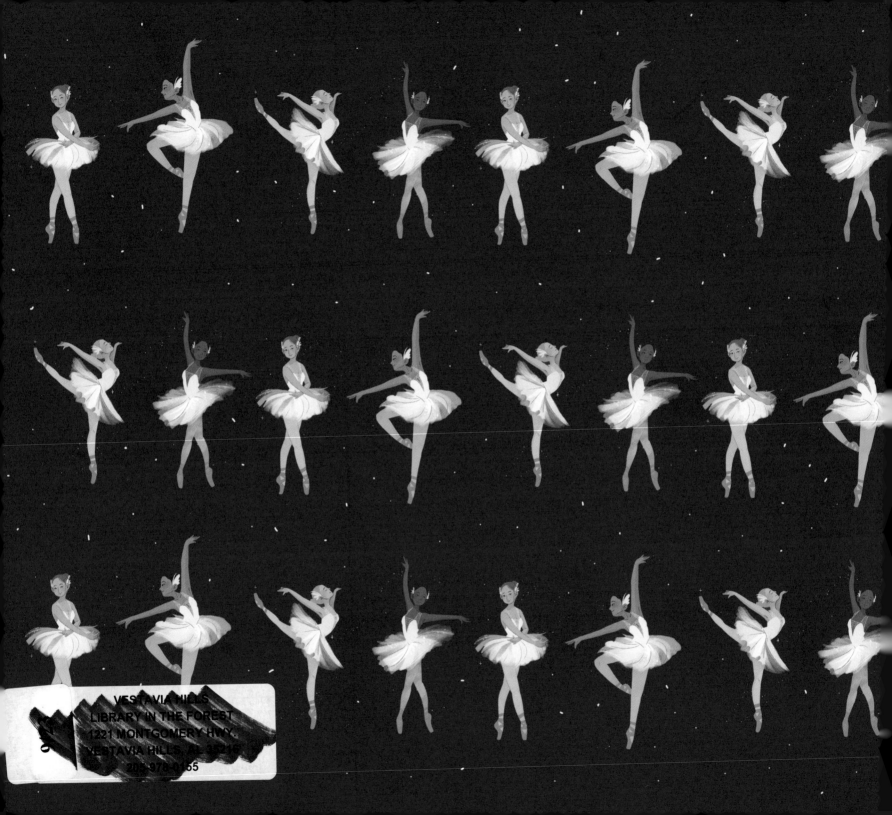